Haunting the Hunters

Printed in the United States of America

First Printing, 2013

ISBN 978-1-300-83544-8

H&H Publishing

630 Center St.

Tabor, IA 51653

joshheardbooks@ho

Table of

Preface

Chapter One: Villisca

Chapter Two: "Mr. S"

Chapter Three: Brian

Chapter Four: Chupacabra

Chapter Five: Who's Haunting Who?

Chapter Six: Beyond Broadcasting

Chapter Seven: Black Eyed Kids

Chapter Eight: Ghost Stalkers (Safety First)

Chapter Nine: "Proper" ways to investigate

Chapter Ten: Wrap up

For my uncle, Todd and my uncle, Danny; both of whom were

taken from us far too soon.

Haunting

the

Hunters

Preface

As paranormal investigators, or even those of us who want to become paranormal investigators, we tend to develop certain relationships with the locations we investigate. For those of you seasoned veterans out there, you know what I'm referring to. These locations touch us in certain ways. All the way down to our very souls. These locations stick with us and can even "haunt" our own dreams while we sleep at night. We all have a place or even places like this as investigators. And trust me, the more and more you investigate; the more and more locations begin to affect you in this way. I want to get into some of these spooky locations that leave an imprint on our lives and can forever change who we are as investigators. This will be the premise for the entire book. We will explore certain locations that have touched me in one way or another all while telling some really chilling tales in the process.

Before I really get rolling here, I should give some form of back-round information regarding myself and certain members of the team of investigators that I was a part of. I have been researching the paranormal ever since I was an adolescent. At this point, that is truly the better portion of my life. I enjoy investigating and have only recently found my love for writing about my experiences. I am what you would call a "believer" in the supernatural; however, I am also a guarded skeptic. All that this means is that I try to question every little thing. If I am left with some form of evidence that I cannot explain away in some way, then it is possible that what I just experienced was paranormal.

The members of this team that will be a part of this book are all from when I was a member and the founder of the Iowa Western Ghost Hunters group in Council Bluffs, IA. The team was my brother, James, and my friends, Mike,

Blake, and Nathan. If you have read my previous book, then you may know these guys fairly well. Anyone else who was involved didn't really care to be put into a book. I'm fine with that. To be quite honest with you, I understand. Paranormal investigating has been thrust into the mainstream lately, but it's still not something that we normally talk about at the office water cooler. Unless you're me, I guess. I talk about this stuff anywhere I get the chance to, and to whoever wants to listen. I am also one of those brutally honest people who will tell it like it is. I kept a ton of secrets to myself for a very long time, and it wasn't until I wrote that last book, that I let most of those stories go. I have to tell it like it is. I really don't know another way of telling a story. And, let's be honest here, if I haven't developed a sensor in my 31 years on this planet so far, why the hell would I start now? So let's get into these locations that have left their mark on me in some way or another. Enjoy.

Chapter One

One such location that really struck a chord with me was the Axe Murder House in Villisca, IA. This house was built back in 1868. It wouldn't become the property of J.B. Moore until 1903. J.B. Moore was a successful businessman who ran an implement dealership in the town of Villisca. As the story goes, J.B., his wife Sarah, their four children Herman, Katherine, Boyd, and Paul, and two friends Lena and Ina Stillinger had all attended a church service on the evening of June 10th, 1912. Once church was over, the group of eight went back to the Moore's house where they all settled down for the evening. What they all didn't realize was that this would be the final time they would all close their eyes, the final time they would all wish each other a goodnight, or even tell one another "see you in the morning."

There are many different tales as to what events had gone on that fateful night, but one fact remains; there were eight bodies discovered the very next day. A neighbor of the Moore family had become concerned due to the fact that she hadn't seen any activity from the Moore house all morning long. This was certainly an oddity. J.B. was always an early riser on account of his business that he needed to keep afloat. Sarah also was an early riser with house work and other chores to keep a proper house up. The lack of activity concerned the neighbor so much, she went as far as to try and peek through some of the windows of the Moore house but to no avail. The house was locked, shades drawn, and an odd stillness greeted the poor woman who was only concerned for the well-being of her neighbors. She immediately got in contact with the local authorities, voicing her concern they assured her they would come and take a look. Whoever was the first to enter the house literally walked into a scene that can only be described as horrific. Everyone was in their beds still. Only they weren't resting soundly; they were all dead. It is said that J.B. was the only person of the eight that was killed with the sharp side of the axe. Everyone else, it would seem, was bludgeoned to death with the dull, thicker side of the weapon. This was truly a horrible way to die. Not to mention that six of the victims were only children, the oldest child being Herman who was all of 11 years of age.

One oddity surrounding this case was that whoever did the killing covered the mirrors in the bedrooms with sheets either before, or directly after killing the family. This activity raises questions with some. Why would someone display such odd behavior? As if killing eight innocent people wasn't enough, the killer covered the mirrors in the bedrooms. Why? Some say that this monster of a person couldn't stomach seeing himself in such a way. A person truly losing grips with reality. Others say that they would sometimes cover mirrors so that spirits didn't get trapped within the glass, and lose their way to the afterlife. This is not a very big theory, but one that does hold some credence to it.

The most horrifying thing that surrounds the Villisca case is that the case, still to this day, remains open. That's right, no one was ever charged with murdering eight innocent people. There was one person who did confess to killing the Moore family and the two Stillinger girls on the night of June 10th. His name was Reverend George Kelly. Reverend Kelly was a traveling minister who was also known for being a "peeping Tom." As I said before, Kelly did confess to the murders, but no one took him seriously. He was seen more as a kook than anything else. It is said that his confession made a mockery of the legal system. He was, however, tried twice. The first trial resulted in a hung jury, and the second jury acquitted him of all charges.

There are around seven or eight others who were thought to have possibly played some role in the murder of the Moore family, but there was simply not enough evidence to convict anyone. For a moment take yourself back to the early 1900's. The town of Villisca was, and still is, what we would all consider a small town. Now I think I know a thing or five about small towns being as I grew up in a town of around 300 residents. In small towns, news will spread like a wildfire on a hot, dry June afternoon. Once news was spread about the small town of Villisca, people had to see it for themselves. This was not like the police investigations of today, mind you. There was no shinny "caution" tape strewn about warning passersby of a crime scene. People from the town who had no affiliation at all with the police department were walking directly inside the Moore house to take a closer look for themselves. By the time everything was said and done there were dozens of folks who had taken their own mini tour of "Horror Land" thus disrupting a crucial part of investigating; gathering evidence. There would be absolutely no way of telling what items in the house had been disturbed, let alone any other evidence that may have come into play.

That moment literally murdered any chance of finding the true killer, just as he had killed the Moore family.

Growing up, I had heard all the stories of the Villisca Axe murder House. I always enjoyed a good ghost story anyways. Of course, I didn't realize back then how much of an impact that small house would have on me as an adult. All I knew about in adolescence was there were a lot of dead bodies found in that place……… and that was cool. Any teenage boy would agree with me on this one I believe. But it wasn't until I had an opportunity to actually investigate the house itself that I truly realized the terrible crime that had ensued nearly 100 years prior.

I am a *very* thorough investigator. I want to know everything that I possibly can know about an investigation. This includes the Who, What, Why, When, and How of everything. Sometimes this can be a good trait to have, and other times it almost means more to a case, or a client to come up with truly pertinent evidence that the investigator had no prior knowledge of. Regardless of how you feel on that subject, I did my homework when it came to Villisca. I could recite almost any piece of knowledge about that location. Good information to have but, in retrospect I guess I may have over-done it a smidge.

My brother and I shared a dorm room together at Iowa Western Community College in Council Bluffs, Iowa. He was also a big investigator such as me, and my close group of pals. We were all a part of a ghost hunting group that my friend, Mike and I started while we were at college. As a group on campus and with recognition from the college, we were granted a certain amount of money to spend how we saw fit as a group. We of course thought that our money would be best spent on an overnight stay in Villisca. Can you blame us? There are tons of groups out there who would kill for a chance to investigate one of the most haunted houses in America.

We had been planning this trip for what seemed like forever. Everything was ready and in place. We had people divided into specific teams, camera placements, voice recorder placements, and even specific time frames that certain teams would be in the house. We were set and ready for a full out investigation. The day finally came, and, of course, something went wrong. For those of you who aren't familiar with Murphy's Law……. Look that up. It basically states that *anything that CAN go wrong WILL go wrong.* And why should this time be any different?

I was sick. Not like, "I'm going to wretch all over the floor," but sick enough to feel my entire body ache and my head feeling as if it was stuck in some mid-evil torture device. I was pretty sure it was a cold that had hit me sometime over the past 12 hours or so. Regardless of how I felt, I was still making this trip. Come Hell or high water, I would be there investigating just the way I thought an investigation should be conducted.

We arrived at the museum in Villisca per our instructions and met Darwin Linn, the owner of the house. He initially gave us a brief history of the place and we watched a short film on the murders. He then took us to the house and gave us a nice tour of the place. One thing is for sure, Darwin really knew his stuff when it came to the history of the house. After only about 30 minutes or so, Darwin gave us a key to the house and asked us to drop it off at the museum in the morning. He then wished us luck and closed the door behind him. We were officially on our own; ready to place cameras and other equipment and begin our investigation of the Villisca Axe Murder House.

"He didn't stick around too long," Nathan began with a chuckle.

"Not a chance. He doesn't like being in the house after the sun sets. Not that he necessarily believes in the paranormal, he would just rather not find out if it is true or not," I rebutted, knowing a little more about Darwin than the average person. Darwin and I had spoken on many different occasions. Hell, he was an acquaintance of my family who lived in Villisca.

Needless to say, we were all pretty amped up, ready for anything to happen. I was still feeling under the weather, despite all the Day Quill I had ingested prior to our arrival. I felt it best to take a nap. Yeah I know how crazy it sounds to want to sleep when one of the biggest investigations of my career was going on right around me. I still needed to be on my best game. So I told the group that I was going to take a short nap and recharge my "batteries" for a while. I specifically remember telling Nathan to wake me up if anything noteworthy was going on. Nathan gladly obliged and I took to the couch in the main living room area of the house. Mind you, this is one of the most uncomfortable couches that you will ever sit, let alone sleep on. The couch, surprisingly did the trick, and within a few brief minutes, I was asleep. Most likely, I had OD'd on the Day Quill, something that has been known to happen before to me.

I didn't dream of a thing during my time on the hard couch, which is positioned directly outside of what is known as the "blue room." This is the same bedroom that Lena and Ina Stillinger were sleeping in when they met their untimely demise. This is also the only bedroom that is located downstairs in the house. Like I was saying, I didn't dream a thing. I was exhausted and was sleeping very soundly when I remember being tickled by someone. This was really annoying to me, so I rolled myself over and swung my arm as if to swat at whoever was the tickler in question. But my arm fell hard and only met with the unforgiving side of the couch that I was resting on. My eyes immediately opened only to be greeted by an empty room. I could hear the footsteps and low murmurs of my fellow investigators upstairs doing their normal sweeps it would seem; so why or how was it that I was being tickled?

Sweeping my brain for all that "useless" information that I keep stored for a rainy day, I remember hearing stories of Lena and Ina being the tricksters of the group and would, on occasion, tickle or even yank on a pant leg or two. Did I just encounter one of the Stillinger girls pulling a prank on me? Was one of the girls trying to make contact with me? Did they have something to say? I'm not saying yes or no. That is for you, the reader, to decide. Regardless of what had just happened to me and woke me out of a great sleep, some very interesting developments were going on directly above my head. I heard heavy and very, very labored footsteps coming down the stairway which is located right off the kitchen when you first enter the house. It was Nathan coming to wake me up.

"Um, Josh. You should really see this," Nathan's voice was shaking with excitement. He was giddy for sure, but still trying to remain as professional as possible.

"What's going on?" I said, still trying to wrap my head around what just occurred with me."

"You better just come take a look."

I hurried behind him. We raced up the steps. I, still groggy and out of sorts a little, and took an immediate left-hand turn when we reached the top. We then raced down the small hallway to the room at the end of the hall where the rest of the children were sleeping on that fateful night. What I saw next was nothing short of amazing. There was a group of three other people sitting in a half circle, rolling a ball to the open side of the circle, only to have the ball stop and then roll back to one of the team members. This was truly a huge step for me as an investigator. The team had not only made contact with the other side, but they were literally "playing catch" with it. I stood in awed silence for what seemed like an eternity. I then piped up a little and asked a question of my own.

"Can you roll the ball to your favorite person in the circle?" I wasn't expecting a response at this point. I was still curious to see how bad the floor slanted.

The ball was stopped at the time of my questioning. It then remained still for another 10 seconds or so until it moved again and began rolling towards Mike. I was blown away at this moment. This was such an incredible step for all of us as a team. We were receiving intelligent responses from an entity. This is one of those moments that paranormal investigators dream of. Making contact and actually getting responses from the other side.

Side Note:

That incident was what we call an "intelligent" type of haunt. It is only called intelligent because it can interact with you, and possibly answer questions that you may ask, or do certain things that you ask it to do. In other words, the spirit is "intelligently" interacting with you. Another such type of haunting is called "residual." Residual means that whatever it is can happen over and over again. This is similar to a DVD that you may pop in, or a CD that you merely put on repeat. The kicker is that usually when dealing with a residual haunt there is a trigger that has to be put in place before it can actually happen and manifest itself. This may be a certain date, time, weather pattern, or even moon phase. Whatever triggers it then allows the haunting to play itself out. Think of it like a movie that is being played over and over again. Let me give you a scenario

real quick:

It's October 14th, 1973. Our two subjects are Bob and

Susie. Bob and Susie are married. They love each other very

much, but they fight a lot because Bob likes to drink too much

alcohol. Susie calls him on it on this particular night and Bob

loses his temper. He then takes his glass and half empty bottle

of scotch and throws it as hard as he can against the wall. *There

is a lot of emotion running through the atmosphere at this

time. So many emotions are now in play like anger, frustration,

concern, and carnal fear on Susie's part.* Now, as the theory says,

heightened emotions can leave their own mark on the

atmosphere. This now is coming full circle to present day when

a new family moves into Bob and Susie's old house and begin to

experience odd things. In fact, every October 14th there is a

distinct sound that comes from one certain room. It sounds like

glass is breaking, although upon inspection, nothing is out of

the ordinary. That one happening from years prior has burned itself into the atmosphere and will replay itself every October

14th. Kind of weird huh? In some cases, people have seen people

that are dressed in period type clothing simply walk past them or

even through walls and not react in any way to the world around

them. So a residual haunt will not and cannot interact with you

in such a way that an intelligent haunt can and will.

So back to the case in Villisca, we were all stunned. There was no real explanation as to why or how this was going on. Within ten minutes the activity had subsided, but little did we know that the house itself was gearing up for another of the mysteries that surround this location.

We all decided to take a little break. This was simply to clear our own heads as to what had just happened so we could continue on with our investigation in as professional a manner as possible. After a short break we headed back into the house. The atmosphere inside the house felt different somehow. It was heavier inside the house and not at all welcoming. We all could sense the overbearing feeling of evil at this moment. It was as if the "mood" of the house itself had changed. I instructed everyone to place their recorders and video cameras back in their original spots and let them roll. Something big was about to happen.

A little earlier I mentioned the different types of hauntings that certain locations can show us; Intelligent and

Residual. This is where the Villisca house really comes to life. Along with the intelligent haunting, there is also a residual haunt that will kick in at certain times. We didn't realize when this would ever occur until it happened again, and again, and again.

The Villisca house is located very close to railroad tracks and there are still trains that will roll through Villisca at all hours of the day and night. For our little group, this is what triggered the residual haunt. Whenever the train would roll through town, it would blow its whistle and make it somewhat difficult to hear what was being said inside the house. Now this is only speculation but, what if the sound of a train was used to the killer's advantage? The noise caused from the train would make it quite a bit easier to travel from room to room and slaughter whoever may be lying in those beds. Again, this is only a theory that we all came up with during our investigation. It would help lend a little more credence to the fact that the mood of the house would change so dramatically right as a train would pass through Villisca.

One of the most unsettling thoughts to me now, as a father, and simply as a human being, is considering this residual haunt. Technically speaking, if the residual haunt triggered every time that a train would pass through the town, then that would indicate that those innocent people are also being murdered over and over on a daily basis. I hate this thought, but I also can't help but to entertain it.

There are many claims out there as to where the killer was when the Moore family returned from church that evening. Some say that the killer was already inside the house, patiently waiting for the family to retire for the evening. There are others who suggest that the killer simply happened upon the Moore residence and the family may have simply been in the wrong place at the wrong time. This would sit a little better with those who didn't think the murder was pre-meditated. I am of the impression that the killer was inside the house as the family got home that night. I also believe that he was in hiding somewhere in the house waiting for that perfect moment to strike. Maybe he was patiently awaiting the train for the extra noise cover. None of us really know, do we? Truth be told, we probably won't ever know what truly transpired on that night.

Another big controversy surrounding the case is if the killer acted alone, or if he had a helper……… or maybe two. While investigating at the house, we set a camera at the top of the stairs, which is inside the master bedroom, facing down the hall, shooting directly into the children's bedroom. Looking from that angle, there is a small "crawl space" or attic door on the left hand side of the hallway, about halfway down. With the camera in place and rolling, we were all downstairs conducting more tests. You can clearly hear our voices on the recording. Mostly its murmurs and slight chuckles at times, but it is quite clear that we were not on the same level of the house as the camera.

At one point on the recording, you clearly see the crawl space door swing open and come to a rest in the "full open" position. Almost immediately after the door comes to a halt, you can clearly see three separate "disturbances" that appear to be walking out of the door. I only call them disturbances because I can't find the right words to describe them. They look as if they are long, slender, vertical, wavy lines that "walk" out of the door. After only a brief moment, you can see these same disturbances re-enter the crawl space and the door slams fairly hard directly behind them giving us another great piece of evidence from the Villisca house.

More great pieces of evidence that are easily gained from Villisca are the EVPs. EVP stands for Electronic Voice Phenomenon. These are the disembodied voices of the dead that we can't hear with our own ears at the time of the recording. It is theorized that the reason for this is because ghosts are operating on a different frequency than what we are. It also helps that our microphones on our digital recorders are super sensitive. On occasion you can sometimes hear the voices as they are being said from the entity. This is rare for me, but it can happen. I have friends in this field that can pick up on a lot of spirit voices as they are happening. I wish I could have that ability. Maybe I just listened to my music way too loud as my mother warned me not to do in my youth.

Over the years we have gained some really compelling EVPs from the Axe Murder House. One immediately springs to mind; Nathan was investigating the "Blue Room" downstairs. He asks a series of questions, one of which was asking the entity for his/her name. After he posed the question about nine to ten seconds pass before you can clearly hear what sounds like a little girl say, "I'm Ina." This was very exciting to hear, simply for the validation of the spirit announcing itself as Ina in the same room where Ina Stillinger took her last breath.

Nathan has always had pretty good luck when it comes to getting EVPs. Another he got from Villisca is a voice that asks three questions, one right after the other. To me it sounds as if it is a woman's voice. The voice simply says, "Who are you? What do you know? Why did you come?" Could this be Sarah Moore's voice asking all of these questions merely from the role of a protective mother? I guess anything is truly possible. What's truly odd is that in the same audio file you can hear another voice directly on top of "Sarah's" voice saying "Come on out, Paul." As you know, Paul is one of the children whose life was cut short that night as well.

There are many things that keep me going back to Villisca, IA for paranormal research. For one thing, that house never seems to disappoint. Another reason is that I have become attached. Not attached to the doors slamming, EVPs, or even the delicious cold chills that I receive when a spirit is close. I am attached to that family. I have done so much research on that location that I almost feel like I knew the family that once lived there. I too have developed a giant sense of empathy for the children there. I can't imagine what it would be like to have your life end at such a young age. It sickens me to my very core.

So many places, like Villisca, touch us on so many different levels. We almost start to feel the same pain as the victims in this particular case. We, at the very least, sympathize with them and those whom it affected.

On a personal note, I would like to say a very special "Thank You" to Darwin Linn, former owner of the Villisca Axe Murder House. Darwin passed away a few years back, and I never got a chance to thank him in person for introducing me and sharing with me his amazing house. It truly has changed who I am as a person, and as an investigator. Darwin, my friend, you are truly missed.

The Villisca Axe Murder House

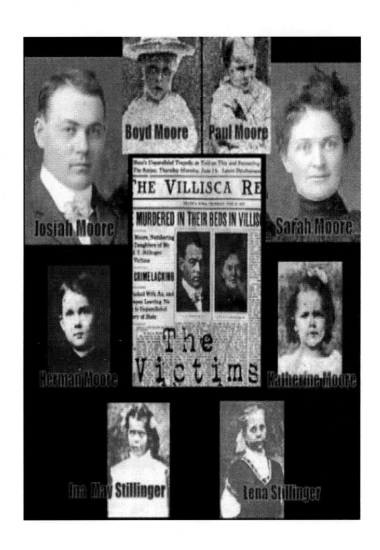

The Victims

The uncomfortable couch

Side Note:

Conducting an EVP session is really quite simple. Start with general, generic questions that you may ask anyone whom you come across in your day to day life. Some good starting points are:

- "Is there anyone here who wants to talk with me?"

- "What is your name?"

- "What year is it?"

- "Does it make you mad that I am here?"

Always remember to leave adequate time in between your questions. This is to allow the spirit enough time to actually answer you. I usually wait 20-30 seconds between my questions.

Another good technique to use is the "Burst Session."

Burst Sessions are short, three to five minute EVP sessions. Only

ask a few questions. The point of having such a short session is

so that you can review the audio evidence immediately

afterwards and it won't take you all day to do so. This way if

you do come up with something credible, you can go right back

to asking questions that are more along those same lines.

Chapter Two

Like Villisca, there are many more places that we are going to visit that can influence us and who we are. Sometimes they aren't even houses at all. In this particular case, I am speaking of a lonely road in the middle of nowhere that was once the horrific scene of a suicide. For this story I am keeping most of the information to myself as to protect certain parties involved.

This particular case was/is a tough one. Throw history out the window entirely. There are no records, only heresy and eye witness accounts. As the story goes, a man, for this story we will call him "Mr. S," was in a very dark place in his life, and decided to take matters into his own hands. With that thought, he ended his own life. He had driven his truck out to a desolate road completely canopied with this leaves and wilderness, parked the vehicle, and then shot himself in the head. What made him do it? We can only speculate at this point. As I said before, no one is truly sure of why "Mr. S" did what he did. What I do know is that he was hidden well enough from any passersby; that his lifeless body sat there literally for one full week. This is terribly tragic and a damn shame that he wanted to end his life in this way.

For whatever reason, I was told about this place and on one evening, decided to go check it out for myself. I brought only a few of my "toys" with me on this trip. I had an EMF detector, and a digital recorder. For those of you keeping track at home; an EMF detector is a tool that measures for fluctuations in the electro-magnetic field. In other words, it looks for weird spikes of electrical energy that seems displaced.

It was well past dark on this night. I had only one other person along for the ride, and that was Mike. We initially arrived at the location and I parked my car around the same area of where "Mr. S"'s body and vehicle were discovered. Whenever I investigate any location, I like to really get a feel for the place first. I take in the vibe as much as possible when I first arrive at a location. I believe that you can tell a lot by a place simply from using your own natural, god given senses. Given this, Mike and I rolled down our windows, killed the engine, and sat silently in the car. After only a few minutes I started to feel like there was something around us. This is when Mike and I began to ask the easy "ice-breaking" type of questions. Things like "Is there anyone here," or "What is your name?" Sometimes these questions deliver results, and other times they simply don't.

As we sat there asking questions, I asked a very specific one. I asked the spirit to please make a noise, or to somehow let us know it was around. After I posed the question, only a few moments passed before Mike and I felt a fairly strong jolt. It felt as if someone had pushed the back of my car. This was a little alarming simply because I was expecting a tap on the car door or even the hood, but this was fairly strong. So me, being the guarded skeptic that I am, ask the spirit if it could please do it again. A few seconds passed and Mike and I felt the same jolt as we did before.

At this point I was in awe, but also wanted to see for myself if anyone was around messing with us. Mike and I then got out of the car to investigate a little further. We walked back towards the rear of the car only to find nothing there. I then took it upon myself to look under the car. Again there was nothing. Mike suggested we sit back in the car and try to get the spirit to repeat the activity. So we climbed back in the car, situated ourselves, and began asking the same line of questions. This time there was nothing. There were no taps, no knocks, and certainly no shoves to the back of the car. Even the feeling that I was experiencing before had subsided. The energy was gone. After another 30 minutes of getting no activity, we decided to call it quits for the night. The funny thing is, Mike and I never once used one piece of equipment that we brought that night. We agreed that there was something odd that was going on around that area, and thought we should come back sometime in the near future.

This is one of the main things to pay attention to if you are considering paranormal investigations as a hobby. When things happen, they happen fast and are usually very short lived. I believe that this is due to an entity's lack of energy. Entities need energy to manifest themselves or even to move objects or knock on a wall. If there is not sufficient enough amounts of energy in the area for the entity to draw from, the activity will die out.

Side Note:

EMF stands for Electro-Magnetic Field. It is theorized that ghosts are made up of nothing but energy. This is why we use the EMF detectors. These detectors measure for subtle fluctuations within the electro-magnetic field. So if I am walking around, for example, and have a constant reading of a 0 to a 1 on my EMF detector, and it suddenly shoots to a 5 or a 6, this could be a possible spirit trying to manifest itself. This is given that certain steps have been taken by you, the investigator.

One thing to realize is that a lot of things give off EMF readings. Computers, televisions, microwaves, wall sockets, and the list goes on and on. One reason we do our investigations in the dark, is because these specific items are turned off, therefore giving off no EMF readings. But remember that there are active and live wires that run through and under houses too. It is very important to always know your location inside and out before jumping out of your shorts thinking you have something paranormal going on.

Sometimes these wires will emit such a large EMF level that it can affect humans on the physical level. High amounts of EMF can be dangerous and, if we are exposed to them long enough, we can begin to feel anxious, scared, and even nauseous. The high EMF can create what is commonly referred to as a "fear cage." This is an area of high EMF that you would be exposed to for an extended period of time causing you to sometimes feel like you are being watched, or even making you feel paranoid.

After a few days had gone by, I told a good friend, Ron about the location and the activity that Mike and I had encountered. Ron has been a great friend to have in this field. He has a lot of knowledge on the paranormal. We both like to swap tales with each other, and even go investigating together. Ron thought this case was interesting enough, so he and I traveled out to the narrow, dirt road together. I parked the car in the same spot as I did when I was with Mike. On this occasion, however, Ron and I both brought our toys with us, and we had every intention of using them. We brought EMF detectors and digital recorders that I thought may come in handy for trying to measure and record any odd happenings.

This time, Ron and I decided to get out of the car and sweep the area with our equipment. We were using our EMF meters and we were both receiving some pretty interesting "hits" on the instruments. We walked back off the dirt road a small distance and began to follow a tree line that hugged the road and created a fairly spooky canopy of sorts.

Ron and I had been walking for maybe two minutes when I felt a sharp pain on my left shoulder blade. It hit me with enough force that I knew, whatever it had been, was thrown at me. I then was met with the familiar sound of hard metal hitting the ground. I recognized the familiar "ting" that came along with the thud. Ron didn't know what had just happened.

"Something just hit me in the shoulder," I had said in a fairly alarmed type of way.

Ron only looked at me. I know he didn't buy into what I was saying. Why should he? If it were me in his shoes, I would be questioning it too. I asked him to shine a flashlight on the ground. I scanned the dirt, grass, and twigs until I saw it. There, lying in the soft, cold, grass was a small, metallic wrench. It wasn't anything big by any means, but it was big enough to hurt a little bit when it was chucked at my backside.

"Well I'll be damned," Ron said. Now he did believe me and what had just happened.

The meters were dead as far as readings go, and nothing else seemed to be going on so we decided to walk back to the vehicle. We were only about 40-50 yards away from the car when we began the trek back. I was still fairly shaken up about what just happened to me. I was going over it and over it in my head all the way back to the car.

"What is all of this?" Ron remarked as we neared the car.

I looked and saw the top of my car covered in what looked like dirt. Getting closer still, I could tell that it was, in fact, dirt. Big clods of dirt had been thrown all over the top of my car. What was odd about this situation was that you could clearly see that these clods of dirt had been thrown.

There was a point of impact, and then the familiar V-shaped splatter that lie with it. The clods had all come from the same direction, as we could tell from the splatter marks and patterns of the clods. How could this be? Ron and I, to my knowledge, were the only ones out here at this moment. The closest house is a farm house about a mile away from where my car was parked. Could it be that someone was out there at the same time? Sure, it's possible. I will tell you that whoever may have done this was on foot because I could have seen and heard a vehicle approach from a half a mile away. So that part remains a mystery to Ron and me.

I have been to this place many different times since Mike and I's initial visit. Sometimes this location is very active, obviously, and other times it has been stagnate. I found this place so interesting and intriguing that I decided to do paranormal investigator training on the property. If something were to happen, that would be great. If nothing were to happen, I would be happy with that too. The main thing I wanted was for the trainees to get familiar with the equipment and the thought of tracking down a disembodied spirit. And most of the time, nothing happens at all. But on those rare occasions that something does happen, I'm happy to say, that we are all ready for it.

There is obviously something weird or "para" normal going on out at this location. It holds a special place in my heart because of its gruesome history. I try to feel for these spirits as much as I possibly can. I can't imagine being so depressed that I wanted to take my own life. End everything in the blink of an eye. But what comes next? Are you then trapped in that location? It's possible, I guess anything is possible. I have seen way too many odd things happen to not believe that. But think of the amount of sadness and sorrow one must be feeling in that moment. That moment when the gun is loaded, cocked, and aimed directly at you is the crucial moment that I am talking about. What would be going through your mind? That is when all the bad things flood you. The hurt feelings, the pain, the sorrow, the anger, the guilt all comes at you in one huge wave. And then, it's over. What is left at that location? All those feelings that flooded you before the final moment are left, burned into the atmosphere. This is why locations such as this stick with me. The energy is raw and as real as you can ever experience.

Chapter Three

We are going to take another trip back in time for a bit. We are now going back to my college days at Iowa Western in Council Bluffs, IA. What a great time this was in my life. I was pursuing paranormal happenings on a daily basis and loving every second of it. Now those of you who know me realize that when I set my mind to something, it consumes me until I get the outcome I want. While in college, this meant that I had to choose one thing or another. My possible choices were ghost hunting or grades. I chose ghost hunting simply due to the fact that I wanted answers as to what happens to us after we die. It was as if I was on a mission to find answers, but really not getting anywhere significant. Because of my obsession with this field, my grades suffered greatly. Looking back on those days, I am regretful that I didn't pay more attention or attend more classes, but at the same time, I wouldn't trade the experiences that I had with the other side for a single damn thing.

I was an R.A. (That stands for Resident Advisor.) What this meant was that I had to hold floor meetings with everyone who lived on my floor, do room checks on occasion, and mostly make sure members of the opposite sex were off the floor by a certain time of night. So in all actuality, I was a babysitter for 20 year olds. But there was a very nice perk to all of this babysitting. I was granted an entire dorm room to myself, meaning more room for all my geeky, ghost hunting equipment. Not to mention a sweet video game set up with a sound system that would have put Aerosmith to shame. Regardless of my tunes and games, I now had the freedom to come and go as I pleased without even a second thought as to whom I may be waking up at 5 AM as I'm stumbling into the door.

I remember Christmas break one year that sticks out the most in my mind. As and R.A. I was expected to be back a few days before the rest of the regular student population was expected back. As I walked into the building I was met by a familiar face, Tyler. Tyler was the "head honcho" of the dormitory at that time. Tyler was a good dude and even went as far as to become the sponsor for the ghost hunting group that Mike and I had started while on campus.

"Ho Ho Ho," I began.

"We should probably talk," Tyler was more serious in this moment than I had ever seen him. We walked back to the dormitory offices, all the while I was expecting to lose my job for whatever reason. I usually picture the worst case scenario first.

"So, what's up," I asked in a rather serious manner.

"One of the residents on your hall passed away last night," Tyler stated in his normal, mater-of-fact tone.

"Which resident was it?"

"It was Brian," he said. "Car accident, he was in the wrong place at the wrong time."

My initial thoughts went immediately to Brian's family. For God's sake the kid was only 20 years old. This was going to be a huge blow to them.

I got to know Brian quite well since I became an RA. Our rooms were literally right next door from one another so there was always something going on. I can say this now, since I am no longer employed by the school, but my motto for the floor was: "If I don't see it, smell it, or hear it; it isn't happening." The floor residents respected me a little more for this outlook on life. I think their girlfriends did too.

Brian was quiet and kept to himself most of the time. If you know me on a personal level, then you know that I am a pusher. I will talk and talk until I basically force a conversation out of you. So I did have plenty of conversations with Brian and even his father on occasion. This was a terrible blow for all of us on campus. Tyler said that Brian's father and mother would be stopping by to collect his belongings and clear out the room. It was the thought of me being the one having to let them into the room, me being the one to give condolences, and me being the one to help carry out the last of Brian's life. It was all very unsettling for me. Honestly, it was driving me crazy. It is a moment like that when a simple "I'm sorry for your loss" doesn't quite cover it. Their entire world came crashing down in a simple moment of time that happened in an instant.

The time came when Brian's family arrived. Conversation was light but very pleasant. I escorted them to the elevator and showed them to Brain's door. I placed my master key into the lock, turned the key and pressed lightly. We all entered the room, me entering last. It wasn't until that moment that Brian's mother began to cry. I'm sure that seeing Brian's personal belongings was simply too much for her to handle.

"I can't do this. I'm so sorry," she said lightly as she exited the room and ran back for the elevator.

"I apologize," Brian's father began, but I cut him off.

"There is no reason to be sorry. It is a lot to handle and swallow in such a short amount of time," I tried to reason.

He stared at me for what seemed like eternity, then nodded his head, choking back tears and began to grab armloads of clothes. I was right behind him too, lugging Brian's stuff out to his parents' van an armful at a time. Not another word was spoken between us.

The whole process only took about 20 minutes. Brian didn't really have that much "stuff." He did own a lot of clothes though, which was the majority of the carrying. After the final load was packed up, his father reached out his hand for a shake. I gladly accepted and as soon as his hand grasped mine, he pulled me in for a hug. At that moment I wanted to cry like I had never cried before. It was as if I could feel his pain and deep sorrow for only a brief moment. But that brief moment would stick with me for the rest of my life. With that, Brian's parents drove off, leaving campus for good. I know they missed Brian. We all did. None of us knew that we hadn't heard the last from Brian though. He was still around, and he wasn't that far away either.

It was on that evening that some odd things began to happen. Mike had come over to my room for our nightly ritual of video games and Family Guy episodes on Adult Swim. Mike was an R.A. as well which really helped me having such a close friend to hang out with since the rest of the student population would still be gone another two days. While playing a golfing game with Mike, a game in which I was winning by the way, the lights flickered. None of us thought a thing of it. I did take note of the lights flickering; however, no one mentioned anything at the time. Power surges happen all the time and it is our job as investigators not to jump to outlandish conclusions at the drop of a hat.

It was Mike's turn on the game. During his player's backswing another power surge occurred, only this time it was a little more intense. Directly following the flicker, the power went out completely.

"Goddamn it," Mike was wailing. I guess he was a little upset that his game was just shut off. I immediately stifled him with a loud "Ssshhh."

Typically a power outage is not really a big deal considering that the dormitory had a backup generator for just such an emergency, but I knew that something was very wrong with this situation. It was pitch black in my room except for a glow coming from the crack underneath my door. The glow was from the hall lights. The power was still running except for, seemingly my room. I darted across the hall and "keyed in" to my friend Rob's room. I figured no one else was around so why not try and get to the bottom of this. I wasn't going to riffle through Rob's shit; I merely wanted to flip some switches. Just as I thought, the lights turned on in Rob's room. This gave me confirmation that there was only a power problem in my room.

Excellent, I thought to myself.

My door was left open across the hallway where Mike was still waiting for me. I turned and could see Mike plainly. My attention was turned toward Rob's empty room when I heard a slight commotion coming from my room. I saw Mike standing with his arms outstretched in that all too familiar "what the hell?" style. The lights in my room were flickering off and on at this point. Mike was still standing in the middle of the room dumbfounded as to what was going on. Then as soon as the activity had started, it was over.

Mike and I stood there motionless. The lights in my room had restored themselves to their normal state of functioning and all seemed quiet. The whole ordeal lasted only a few minutes, but it seemed like more. From that moment on, I believed that Brian was simply stepping in to say hello to us. That was the last time that Mike and I "heard" from Brian. I know that he is at peace and in a much better place than what he left behind.

Chapter Four

This has a different feel to it than the previous stories thus far. This has to do with an aspect of the paranormal that isn't necessarily "the norm" of the field. This particular chapter has to do with crypto-zoology. Crypto-zoology is the study of strange and unknown creatures. If you think of crypto-zoology, images of the Loch Ness Monster and Bigfoot spring into our heads. This isn't any type of creature like that. This is something that is a little more, blood thirsty. No, I'm not talking about Robert Pattinson either. I'm speaking of the creature that goes by the name "Chupacabra." Chupacabra is a Spanish term that roughly translates to "Goat Sucker" in English. Sound a little weird? I thought so too. But is there anything to this phenomenon?

During my time at Iowa Western I received a phone call from a member of the teaching staff. I had never talked to this person before in my life and found it especially odd that they would be calling me, but no matter. Honestly, I thought that I had done something to piss someone off and this particular professor was the only one with the "testicular fortitude" to actually call me on it.

It was an odd conversation to say the least. The professor asked me and Mike to come and meet with him in his office around noon. Mike and I certainly didn't have anything better to do at that time of the day so we obliged. Sitting down in his cramped office, the professor began to tell Mike and me about an encounter with what he claimed to be a chupacabra.

The professor, in the summer months, volunteered as a camp counselor at a camp for children. I knew of this camp very well, being somewhat familiar with the area. Plus it was only about a 10 minute drive from Council Bluffs. The camp, the professor explained, also was home to a fair amount of livestock. They raised horses, chickens, sheep, and even on occasion, pigs. The professor explained that earlier that very morning, the groundskeeper woke up to do the morning chores and tend to the animals. The only problem was that all of the sheep and one of the horses were dead. This took me by complete surprise, and Mike was speechless.

My initial thought was that some sick person had come in and butchered all of these defenseless animals. I asked about the manner in which these animals met their end to which the professor explained that, "that was the weird part." It seemed that all the animals had been killed, but not a single drop of blood was anywhere to be found. The only evidence of foul-play was two somewhat small puncture wounds in the necks of all the deceased animals. This was sounding more and more like a Dracula-type case to me.

I had to see this for myself. I asked the professor if I could go and examine the animals for myself. The professor of course was on board with that idea and offered to drive Mike and myself out to the camp. Mike refused, saying he needed to go to a class. I, on the other hand, decided to take the professor up on his offer and quickly followed him to his vehicle about 45 minutes later.

I was nervous about this case for some reason. After all, I dealt with ghosts and certain things that go bump in the night. Now I was about to go play CSI on some dead sheep. *What the hell was I getting myself into,* I thought to myself as we came upon the camp grounds.

Getting out of the vehicle I was instantly greeted with the amazing aroma of nature. It was only the professor and me at that moment. He pointed in a general direction, and we both began to walk towards "the scene of the crime." I noticed that the professor didn't say much since we arrived at the camp. There was something that was definitely troubling him. We came upon the stable area where the animals had been kept. I could already see that there was at least four dead sheep lying on the ground. Approaching more and more I could also tell that there was no carnage whatsoever. It was just as he explained. No blood, just dead animals.

I wanted to jump the fence and take a closer look for myself when I heard another set of footsteps coming up behind me. I turned and saw the groundskeeper walking up towards the professor and me. He looked tired as hell and almost as if he hadn't slept in days. Of course finding all of these dead animals at once might have had something to do with that.

We shook hands and made introductions and then I began to question the groundskeeper. His voice was trembling; his hands were shaking as he recounted what had transpired earlier that day. He had told me exactly what the professor had explained earlier that day to me. And lying directly in front of me was the evidence just as they had described.

Taking a closer look at the sheep, you could clearly see two very distinct puncture wounds in the neck of the animal. And, just as they said, no blood could be seen. Now please understand I have never been good with dead animals. I think it is because I think of them as defenseless and pure creatures. They don't give two shits of what society thinks of them or their way of life. So, in essence, they are the exact opposite of humans. This was straight out of a horror movie. I couldn't believe my eyes, but there was all the evidence I needed.

I began to ask the professor what their course of action was going to be. They had already contacted a veterinarian who was coming to dispose of the bodies in the morning. Just as I was about to ask a follow up question I felt a pressure on my arm. It was the groundskeeper who had turned to me, grabbed my arm just above the elbow, and started saying "I knew they didn't want us here."

Okay…….. Now this just took on a whole new kind of creepiness for me.

"Who doesn't want us here?" I asked in such a hesitant way it would have made school-girl laugh.

"They don't. They don't want us here. They never have," the groundskeeper said almost as if he was fighting off tears.

That was it. He was leaving. I was still trying to get to the bottom of this, and off he went. I was not amused at all. First of all, don't start spouting craziness out of your mouth like you're in some Stephen King made for TV movie. And certainly don't just walk off after spouting that crazy crap. It creeps me out!

"Who doesn't want us here?" I asked the professor.

"He claims that the reason the animals died off in such an odd way is due to alien activity."

Now what the hell is a guy to do with that? Am I after a chupacabra, a mythical creature with no concrete evidence to back up, or am I to assume that some alien beings came down and killed a bunch of livestock? Either side was looking pretty bleak to me at that moment. I stood there dumbfounded at what the groundskeeper had just said. Either way was a losing battle for me. I know a lot of investigators from all walks of life. Some have a wide array of equipment at their disposal, and others use nothing more than their own feelings. I respect both approaches. I actually use both approaches on every investigation that I am a part of. But in all of my years of doing this I have never come across one person who is so lucky to have captured evidence of a being or a creature in one sitting. If I was going to do this it was going to take some serious man hours and, of course some serious video surveillance equipment.

Now, as fun as it sounds to go and sit in the middle of the creepy-ass woods all night long, I ended up talking to the professor about my concerns surrounding the case. I didn't want to sound uninterested in the case. I was interested. My main concern was only that no one had ever caught one on camera before. There have been thousands of eye-witness accounts, but no real hardcore evidence. If there is ever a shot of one, it is usually explained away as a dog or coyote with mange or some kind of disease that would alter the appearance of the animal. I didn't want to be in the woods every night for a month trying to get a glimpse of this thing, and that's if it even came back.

On the other hand, if the creepy groundskeeper was right and it was some kind of alien encounter, I would be all over it. Aliens have fascinated me ever since I was a little kid. It has been a subject that not a lot of people take stock in. I think that more people have an easier time believing in ghosts than they do extra-terrestrials. I'm sure that there are many different reasons for this. But from a scientific standpoint, life existing elsewhere isn't only a possibility; it's a mathematical certainty. Only in recent memory experts examining results from the Kepler telescope have identified more than 1,200 planets in orbit around distant stars, 54 of which are a similar size to Earth and in habitable zones from their suns. This means that those 54 planets are in the "Goldilocks Zone." This is an area that is considered to be a "just right" distance from the planet's own sun to support life. Exciting right? And that is only one tiny section of what is actually out in space. It really is a mere fraction. For some, this is terrifying. Thinking about another species of life is enough to send us running for the hills.

Regardless of how much "little green men" terrify us as a race, I didn't find it necessary to spend every night for a month or two simply looking at the stars and hoping to see something anomalous. There are real experts that do that kind of thing for a living. And in the city of Council Bluffs, IA there is a gentleman who is actually a higher-up in the group called MUFON, which is the Mutual UFO Network. These guys really take this stuff serious and are very professional when it comes to investigating UFO's.

I can't believe it myself, but I actually turned down the case. I simply said that there were others out there who were more qualified at dealing with those specific things. They all understood and didn't blame me at all. I did help them in getting in contact with a certain group who did go ahead and take on the case. Honestly, I tend to stick more with the things that go bump in the night other than the things that could have me for dinner.

All of these cases have touched me in one way or another. Every time I drive by these locations or simply hear their names I have something that stirs within me. It's like these places are calling out to me, almost like they themselves are alive. But why does this happen to us? Why is it that certain locations have this kind of affect or draw to us? Is it possible that these places can somehow "talk" to us? This is now our journey and quest for the next few chapters.

Side Note:

Crypto-zoology simply means the study of hidden animals. It is a pseudoscience involving the search for animals whose existence has not been proven. This includes looking for living examples of animals that are considered extinct, such as dinosaurs; animals whose existence lacks physical evidence but which appear in myths, legends, or are reported, such as Bigfoot and Chupacabra; and wild animals dramatically outside their normal geographic ranges, such as phantom cats (also known as Alien Big Cats). The animals that crypto-zoologists study are often referred to as *cryptids*, a term coined by John Wall in 1983. Crypto-zoology is not a recognized branch of zoology or a discipline of science. It is an example of pseudoscience because it relies heavily upon anecdotal evidence, stories and alleged sightings.

Crypto-zoology has been criticized because of its reliance on anecdotal information and because some crypto-zoologists do not follow the scientific method and devote a substantial portion of their efforts to investigations of animals that most scientists believe are unlikely to have existed.

Crypto-zoologists contend that because species once considered superstition, hoaxes, delusions, or misidentifications were later accepted as legitimate by the scientific community, descriptions and reports of folkloric creatures should be taken seriously.

According to Mike Dash, a Welsh historian, few scientists doubt there are thousands of unknown animals, particularly invertebrates, awaiting discovery; however, crypto-zoologists are largely uninterested in researching and cataloging newly discovered species of ants or beetles, instead focusing their efforts towards "more elusive" creatures that have often defied decades of work aimed at confirming their existence

The supposed Chupacabra

Chapter Five

If any of you have read my first book based on a possession case in Maryville, MO you know how terrifying some of these places can be. I mean, watching your one of your best friends get thrown out of a window by something that you can't see may leave you with wet pants. So why is it that I keep going back and doing investigations of that location? Is it passion? Or is it something that isn't quite clicking right in my own brain? Maybe I'm just a glutton for punishment. But there is something about that old chapel that keeps me coming back for more.

It will be at any time of any day, but there it is- an uncontrollable urge to go back and investigate. Again, if you read the first book, we all know that what is there is not something to be toyed with. Certainly, in my mind, it is a demonic force at work within those four walls. I know that whatever is in there hates me, hates my friends, and most definitely does not want us anywhere around. But I'm a very stubborn individual. There is always a small voice inside of me that says *maybe this is the time that you will get that one piece of undeniable evidence.* And that's usually when I begin packing up my car to head out for another tangle with the chapel.

Not only does it happen there, but every time I hear the name Villisca I twinge with delight at the thought of communicating with the afterlife. Many of the "professional" ghost hunters have gone through the house and come out with some very compelling evidence of life after death.

There are even certain locations that I have never been to that I am compelled to investigate. The Myrtles Plantation in Louisiana for example is on my paranormal "bucket list" of places to investigate. This is supposedly one of the most haunted houses in the entire country. And, of course, the Waverly Hills Sanatorium in Kentucky plays host to numerous shadow figures and apparitions. These are only a couple of the million places that I would love to experience for myself. One day I will get there too. I swear it.

But why do these places call out to us? Is there something that is etched in our own personal psyches that allow for such notions to manifest? Or is it the locations themselves that are calling out for our attention?

My biggest feeling towards why we continue to be drawn to these locations lies solely in the experiences we have. I'm going to use myself as an example again. In Villisca, I was able to interact with the other side. I personally watched the physical world around me be manipulated by some unseen force. In Maryville, I have felt pure evil. I watched as an un-godly force took my friend out of a window. I investigate instances of the paranormal and these locations are the closest I have ever been to actually interacting with the other side. They now have a special place in my heart and mind. No matter how terrible, humorous, or chilling some of these experiences, we hold them close. We remember the times when we came close to feeling the other side. This is the best way I can come close to answering why we are so drawn to these places.

Maybe all of these theories are wrong and it is really us who are haunted. Have you ever seen the show "Ghost

Whisperer?" The main character's claim is that locations themselves aren't haunted, but people are. Let's get into this a little more.

Let's say that you have just lost someone who is very close to you. This could be a friend that you have had since childhood, or even a close family member. This person's death is very sudden and unexpected. This constitutes a tragedy in most people's minds. Immediately following their passing, you begin having strange experiences around your home. Lights begin to flicker, electrical equipment will act up seemingly on its own accord, and cold chills seem to greet you around every corner. Could it be possible that what you are experiencing is a spirit? Moreover, is it possible that this is the disembodied spirit of your loved one? Many believe that when we pass away, we don't really go anywhere. Sure we could "cross-over" or whatever you want to call it, or we could stick around. I guess it all kind of depends on your belief structure, doesn't it?

One of my biggest theories is also one that I don't like to vocalize that much. It doesn't sit well with people. If you take any stock in the Bible you believe that when you die, provided you lived a good life, you go to Heaven. Others who have not lived such a good life get sent to Hell. Please make no mistake that I am a Christian, and I do believe that there is a God, but I also think we have a few things wrong. That's understandable right? After all, how long ago was the Bible actually written? And how many times has it been re-written? Let us not forget also that it is an interpretation of another interpretation of a "dead" language that was written thousands of years ago. The gap for error is gigantic.

But the Bible *does* describe one day which has come to be known as "Judgment Day." This is the day when all souls living and dead answer for their sins. So what does that mean? Where are all of our loved ones who have gone before us? If all souls are to be judged on the same day, where does that leave them? Waiting? Walking around? My own belief is that they are around us checking in from time to time. I'm sure that "Joe Schmo researcher" has a zillion other theories as well. Am I saying that I am right? Not a chance. Nor will I ever push this theory on anyone. This is simply my own thoughts and opinions on the matter. Take it all in and build on it. Form your own thoughts.

Any answer or theory simply leaves us scratching our heads even more doesn't it? Welcome to the beauty of paranormal research.

So it is absolutely possible that people can be haunted. It doesn't matter if you are at work, home, church, or out on a date, it is there and can interact with you. These cases seem to be few and far between however. Unlike what the popular TV show would have us believe. When we think of haunted things we usually think of locations. Old houses or abandoned buildings serve as the best settings it seems. These are the locations that just "look" like they may be haunted. And rightfully so by what Hollywood would have us believe a haunted house looks like. But let me be the first to say, that isn't always the case. I have been in newly built places to investigate claims of the paranormal. So what is the reason behind that? Could it be possible that the land itself is haunted? I have heard of several locations in which the land was the cause of the haunting. Here is one of those stories…..

Chapter Six

The team (James, Nathan, Blake, and Mike) and I had been gaining some form of local celebrity around the Council Bluffs, IA area. Honestly, we were taking more flak than anything. Remember, this was back in the day when ghost hunting wasn't considered "cool" yet. "Ghost Hunters" was a newer TV show and paranormal investigations hadn't been thrust into the mainstream as of then.

We were all having a team meeting in the lounge area of the dormitory where we all lived on campus. I got a phone call just as we were about to wrap everything up for the night. It was a disc jockey from one of the radio stations around the area. He found my number through some friends of his that we helped out on a case a while back. He and a co-host were planning on doing a small segment on Paranormal

Investigating. He wanted to know if he and his co-host could follow us around on an investigation. I thought this sounded like a great idea. Now we just needed to figure out where the heck to investigate. Of course we wanted it to be a great location that would be sure to scare the pants off of the DJs.

I thought long and hard about a location. I reeled over and over again about different places that would be sure to "deliver." A thought occurred to me though. What if we could investigate a location that would be new to everyone? This was the best idea in my opinion. There would be no biases in place and therefore, no expectations. This would also give the DJs and the people who were listening, a real feel for how we ran an investigation.

I ran this idea by everyone involved and we began looking for places to go. We scoured newspaper articles, the internet, and even heresy from people on campus. There was everything to poltergeist activity to possible demonic cases. I personally, didn't want to get anyone in harm's way so we scrapped all of the really hardcore cases. This needed to be as simple as we could make it.

Nathan and I were walking around campus one evening and he stopped dead in his tracks.

"Look right there. That's the location."

"The new Arts Center," I asked puzzled. I didn't really think that it would be possible to investigate the brand new building on campus. Not to mention that the college still considered that building their "baby."

"Not the Arts Center itself," Nathan began, "it's what is around the Arts Center."

Now I really was confused. Was he talking about the big open field directly behind the massive structure, or was he talking about the wooded area directly following the open field? Either way I thought he was off his rocker.

"Look," he began, "the Arts Center has already had plenty of claims of weird happenings since it was built. Hell, even while they were building it people were claiming to see and hear odd things. This ground is sacred and has been for hundreds of years. This was the land of the Pottawattamie Indians, a tribe known for their shallow graves. It is no big secret that this used to be their land, and when people began settling on the land they simply built right over the top of some of the Pottawattamie Indian's sacred land."

Nathan had an amazing point. It wasn't necessarily any structure that was haunted it was the land itself that was haunted; haunted by the unsettled spirits of the Pottawattamie tribe that used to inhabit that very same piece of land. I knew that this was our case.

I contacted the radio station and let them know where we would be going and a small amount of information regarding the land's former tenants. They seemed to be pleased with our decision and we began making plans to meet for the broadcast. I was on cloud nine at that moment. We had the case and all we really had to do was show up and do our normal paranormal thing. Of course we would have to do some explaining of the more technical aspects of the investigation to the Disc Jockeys, but for the most part it was smooth sailing from this point on.

The night arrived. It was a clear night, a clear moon shone brightly overhead, and stars cast a perfect blanket of ambiance into the atmosphere. There was even a perfect amount of crispness in the air that night that helped lend its hand to the creepiness. Mike and I were standing on the long, winding sidewalk that eventually landed you right up next to the Arts Center. We had been told to meet the Disc Jockeys in front of the Arts Center around 10:00 that night. Mike and I didn't feel like taking the full arsenal of "ghost toys" that we had at the time, so we decided to simply bring and EMF detector, an audio recorder, and our own good sense. OK, maybe not the good sense part but our *senses* suited us just fine. After what seemed like forever, one Disc Jockey showed up.

"So your partner in crime must have chickened out," I teased the newly arriving DJ.

"He's actually in the studio right now. I am going to patch in through my cell phone and we are going to go live on the air in about 10 minutes."

Now there was pressure. I thought that this was to be a staged "live" event. One that appears like we are investigating to the public but has been edited in certain ways. My biggest concern was language. When on an investigation, sometimes things happen extremely fast and we tend to react without thinking. For most of us, this means cussing and swearing like sailors who haven't seen port in over a year. For me, I have always had somewhat of a problem with my mouth. I apologize, but if something jumps out at me I don't simply greet the situation with a "Oh my goodness." Quite the opposite is the truth. I'm sure that most of you would react in the same way.

There we were. Looking at each other with the same dumbfounded look that you might have if you were just told that they stopped selling your favorite type of liquor at a bar you frequent every Friday night. Stunned silence was all we could muster. We all knew that it was imperative that we delivered a professional and serious investigation. I told the team to take our designated positions. Mike and I would be with the DJ, James and Nathan would be deeper in the woods conducting an EVP session. Our bases were covered. It was time to roll.

"Everyone ready to go, I hope," the DJ was trying to keep a brave face while spitting this particular sentence out. He appeared to be a "tough guy," but definitely jerked his head around at every twig snap or rustling leaf.

"We're good," I said as confidently as I could. All the while I kept telling myself to *act like you're investigating your grandmother's house. Don't swear. Keep a level head and question everything.* This did seem to help calm my nerves a little.

"That is right ladies and gentlemen we are live on the campus of Iowa Western Community College in Council Bluffs doing a live ghost hunt with the paranormal investigative team that resides here on campus," this was all said in that "puking DJ's voice" as I like to call it. You know the kind...... **"YYYYEEESSSSS Friends........This Sunday, Sunday, Sunday!!!"** That type of crap. The next time you listen to the radio pick some of these guys out and really pay attention to how they form their words. I swear it is some of the cheapest entertainment you can find.

I was ready to go. I was amped up and ready to charge. The DJ did ask me initially who I was and where we were. I also gave a brief description of the Pottawattamie tribe and why they would be so upset having all of this civilization literally on top of their ancestors. After a quick little description of toys we would be using, and some of the "lingo" we use, it was time to hunt.

James and Nathan were already set, and doing the EVP session. Mike, the DJ, and I all trekked down farther and farther into the darkness of the wooded area. Now remember, this was a true LIVE investigation. No edit buttons in sight for the poor, unsuspecting DJ. Mike and I began asking questions. The DJ was following both of very closely, and hung on every word. We had officially entered the wooded area, but only at a distance of 40 feet. I stopped suddenly. I had just received my first piece of good news, an EMF spike. It was a small spike, but it was there nonetheless. Mike looked at me with that *I got this* type of look and began asking questions.

"Who are you," Mike began, then waiting the 15 seconds before asking another.

"Are you upset that we are here?"

We didn't know what happened, but I received one of the biggest spikes that you can get on an EMF detector. Whatever or whoever it was, was a very strong entity. Now I should say that when this particular model of EMF detector receives a signal it will make a noise. It can be very loud or very soft depending on how you set the volume on the device. I always set it on loud. My thinking is that if you are investigating with a group of people, sometimes side conversations take place. If a member of the team hears the familiar beeps of the EMF detector, they instantly zip their traps.

As I said before, the spike was big. It was so big, in fact, that it sent my EMF detector into "psycho mode." It was going off like crazy, and it wasn't stopping. I turned to Mike and told him to keep going. Mike couldn't even muster a syllable when another noise happened. This time the noise was a very loud crashing sound from the woods directly beside us.

"Fuck this!" the DJ screamed, turning and running as fast as he could back to the safety of his van.

I didn't know how to react. In all honesty, I was just stoked that I wasn't the one who cussed! I was also a little pissed that he chickened out like that. He literally screamed the "F" Bomb on live radio. It was a magical moment, it truly was. I called James and Nathan in, and we all met up directly behind the Arts Center and discussed how much crazy build up went into this night for nothing. We started back towards the dorms, holding our heads high knowing that no matter what, we didn't run away.

My phone rang as we all were sitting in the commons area of the dormitory. It was the DJ who was at the station running the controls. I asked how everything turned out on his end. He didn't even answer me. He started right in.

"*<u>name deleted</u>* is still pretty messed up. He can't stop shaking, Josh. What the hell happened out there?"

"I got a couple hits on my EMF detector, that's all."

"Well, whatever did happen sent him into a panic. He's truly freaked and doesn't even want to talk about it."

There it was. He was so nervous and afraid before the investigation even started that he had worked himself up beyond any help. Now, I'm not denying that the EMF spikes weren't interesting, but am I calling it paranormal? No way. The crashing sound that came from beside us in the woods was probably nothing paranormal either. It was most likely just a rabbit or squirrel running away because we spooked it. This happens to every one of us at one point or another. Think of it as group hysteria without the group. We build ourselves up with expectations so much that when the occasion presents itself we have no idea of how to handle it personally. In this case the DJ did the only thing that his body would allow him to do. Run away as fast as he could. Fight or flight is very common in what each of us would consider a "high pressure" or "threatening" situation. Put simply, you can stay and fight or run away. It takes a lot of discipline not to run. It took me a long time to train myself to run towards a strange sound rather than away from it. But this is who we are as a species. We all have within us certain limits and boundaries. At that moment in the woods, the DJ found his limit. Not to say that he could experience the same thing a week later and stick it out for 5 minutes longer. But progress is progress.

Chapter Seven

(Black Eyed Kids)

As investigators, we are always looking for "the next big thing." We are trying to find that certain something that we can investigate that will set us apart from all the rest. Most of us begin our searches and journeys into the unknown because of a certain experience that happened to us at some point. But what if we experience something that most people haven't? Something so terrifying that it shakes you to your very soul. Without the information, where do we turn? The internet has plenty of sources on the macabre, but how much of it is factual information? Let me tell you of a recent phenomenon that has a lot of people shaking in their boots. This is truly scary. It frightens the hell out of me personally.

It is a phenomenon known as Black Eyed Kids or BEKs for short.

Imagine yourself home alone. You have just sat down in front of the television or curled up with a great book. You sit, comfortably reading and sipping a glass of wine or bourbon. At this moment you are completely relaxed. All is right with the universe. A sudden knock at the door awakens you from your fantasy world and slams you back into reality. You mark you place in your book, or possibly pause your movie to go answer the door. As you open the front door to your house, you notice three young men, about 13 years old or so. They aren't dressed quite the same as the youth of today, but close enough to pass without raising too many questions. Their request is simple; to come into your house to use the phone, or to get a drink of water, or to use the restroom. But, for some reason there is something that doesn't sit well with you. Their requests are odd, their clothes are a little off, but the most frightening of all is the fact that their eyes are entirely black. No white portion of the eye at all. The color is simply black. And all they want is to gain entrance to your house. What do you think? Let them in? Slam the door in their faces? Listen to this story and then make your decision. This particular story comes to us from someone who goes by, simply "Mikey." Here is Mikey's story:

I had one incident that happened to me last summer while I was driving a semi over the road. I had just pulled into a truck stop inside Billings, Montana. I fueled up, parked the truck in the back of the lot (There are not many truck stops out West. Those that they have are unbelievably huge), then went inside and showered, etc. Come nightfall, I ran out of movies to watch in my truck (I had to wait 34-hours before I could drive the truck again, legally), so I decided on going into the casino that was built inside the

truck stop. I was playing slots and a beautiful American

Indian girl was serving drinks. After quite a few drinks I

started chatting with her on a more personal level. She told

me that her shift ended in a few hours and that she would

be behind the truck stop with a case of beer if I felt like

partying (I did.) I hung around the front of the building, and

when everyone started filing out of the doors, I went around

back to meet her. I couldn't find her, but I found an older,

Mexican woman who seemed to know my name and acted

as if I had just been talking to her inside. I was buzzed, but

not drunk, or stupid. I knew this wasn't the same person.

What also struck me as odd is that she had no personal

belongings besides the clothes on her back. No purse, or

key-ring, nothing. I, starting to feel a little "tripped out"

because of this, began to act like I didn't know her and didn't

want anything to do with her. She became cold and stopped

trying to talk to me... okay, well that was freaking weird.

Here's the totally screwed part. I walk all the way back out to

my truck, climb in the back, change into my sleepwear and

laid on the bunk to re-read a book. Only a few minutes into

the book I hear three loud bangs on the side of my sleeper,

I'm talking "Holy-Crap Your Truck's On Fire! You Have to

Get Out NOW" loud! I opened the curtains and rolled down

the window and saw that the young American Indian

woman I had been speaking with was standing next to my

truck. I immediately picked up something wrong about her.

It wasn't her lack of speech, odd, disheveled look, or rigid body movements. It was her eyes that got to me. Solid black.

I could say that the dark night coupled with a few drinks

could make me think her eyes were black, but I'm not. When

I hit a switch in the back of my truck, the inside lights up

like a baseball stadium. Her eyes seemed to be pulling the

light into them, like miniature black holes, it reminded me of

when a woman wearing mascara cries and she kind of looks

like a raccoon, afterwards. It looked like she had rubbed

charcoal around her eyes. It also felt like my body was

acting of its own accord, my body was screaming at my

fragile psyche to open the door and let her into my truck,

despite the fact that she looked freaking terrifying and

hadn't said a single word to me since meeting her again. I

remember having to choke out the word "No." It reminded

me of when you're on the verge of tears, but you choke

through them to speak to someone. That's how the word "No"

felt when it was passing my lips. I was too damned terrified

to look out my side vents to see if she was still standing

outside, I was too terrified that I might have ended up

looking back into darkness, only to know, in my mind's eye,

that she could be staring right back at me. I've got the shakes

just from remembering that. Oh well, I don't need sleep, just

more coffee.

This is definitely an interesting account of a Black
Eyed *Person*, but not a Black Eyed Kid. There are tons of
stories out there but not many that tell of someone actually
letting these things in. There is one story that is one of my
personal favorites. It does describe a Black Eyed Kid being
let in, however it was entirely by accident. Here is that story:

As the story goes a woman was driving home from

picking her 11 year old son up from school. She decided to

stop off at a gas station to fill up her tank with fuel. After

her gas was pumped she went inside the gas station to pay.

Upon her return to her car, she noticed that she had a new

passenger sitting in her back seat conversing with her son.

The "child" was of about the same age as her son and the two

were chatting. The mother was a little freaked out initially

and noticed something odd about the new passenger. His

eyes were entirely black. The mother quickly got out of the

vehicle and promptly grabbed her son as well, leaving the

Black Eyed Kid still sitting in the car. The mother and son

went inside and called her husband to tell him about the

incident. He could tell from the distress in his wife's voice that this was no laughing matter, and quickly left work to

meet the two at the gas station. In a matter of 10 minutes he

had arrived and, upon inspecting the vehicle, could find no

trace of the mysterious Black Eyed Kid. The only noticeable

thing that was "wrong" with the vehicle was a very

unpleasant odor. That of musty old eggs or sulfur.

The mother was so shaken by this whole experience

that she insisted on not driving her own vehicle, but driving

her husband's vehicle instead. The husband agreed to this

and the family headed for home. The mother and son

arrived home safely, however the husband who was now

driving the mother's car, rolled the car into a ditch only a

few miles down the road. He was hospitalized but only

suffered minor injuries. The vehicle itself was totaled.

This was a very interesting turn of events and somewhat curious at the same time. Could it just be coincidence that this horrible incident happened? It is very possible, but what happened next raises a few eyebrows.

The son who was in the car sitting next to the Black Eyed Kid suddenly fell very ill. He was so ill, in fact that he too had to be hospitalized. The doctors could tell that the boy was in a great deal of pain and in obvious discomfort, but they couldn't find anything medically wrong with him. Once they had an idea of what could possibly be wrong with him, those symptoms would pass and a whole new set of symptoms would appear. He spent a very long time in the hospital, and the medical bills mounted higher and higher.

This continued for months, until one day when all

the symptoms simply disappeared. The boy was discharged

from the hospital and went back home, obviously leaving

the doctors and medical staff scratching their heads. No

further problems have been reported with this family since

those incidents subsided.

Whatever these things may be, one thing is certain.

These claims are fast becoming the biggest anomalies that

we, as investigators have ever seen. Some believe that these

beings are demonic in nature. Others tend to believe that

there is an extra-terrestrial tie to all of these oddities.

Whatever the case may be, we are all still searching for

answers to these strange cases. Dive into all of this a little

more if you wish. There are tons of these claims, each one a

little stranger than the next. But I will tell you this, some of these odd claims date back all the way to the turn of the century.

Chapter Eight

People ask me a lot of questions about investigating. I usually answer any question that is thrown at me with brutal honesty. But one of the main things I do preach is safety. Safety on an investigation is crucial. I can't tell you how many times doing something as simple as a daylight walkthrough of a location has saved my butt. Sometimes these places are literally falling apart around you, and it is your job to not fall, trip, or even die. Know your location in and out because it WILL help you out in the long run.

I currently am a very small portion in a group of young investigators. The "Ghost Stalkers" is what they call themselves. I mostly am there to give advice and to guide. I feel this is my duty as an investigator. I want to pass forward any knowledge that I do have onto these young investigators. I probably feel this need because no one was there to help guide me and help me through all of my paranormal adventures. It is refreshing to be with younger people investigating, simply because we are each teaching one another different styles. We have done many investigations together and have a lot of very big investigations coming up shortly.

This group of young investigators shows a ton of promise. Emma and Kenzie are phenomenal when it comes to gathering information, spirit communication, and using their natural instincts on an investigation. Megan has a special kind of gift. I would consider her to be a sensitive or medium and, with the proper training, will become a serious force to be reckoned with. All in all, the "Ghost Stalkers" are an amazing group of young up and comers.

Now back to the safety issue. One day I was perusing around on a social media website and came across a very interesting story. This particular story came from a town which is about 30 minutes away from my front porch, and lies on a stretch of road know to the locals as "Seven Sisters Road." As the legend goes a man, thought to be a sibling, took his seven sisters out along this eerie stretch of road and hung each one of them separately from trees that ran alongside the road.

Many different tales have been told in regards to this small stretch of road. Tales of ghostly screams coming from nowhere, apparitions that disappear into thin air, and cars losing power and even dying while on the road itself. And now that I have seen this stretch of road for myself, I can say that it is very creepy. I thought that this tale sounded too good to be true. I began trying to do some research on the subject but really couldn't find anything that was solid and factual.

Since there wasn't much information online (go figure) I decided to contact the local police department. I was fortunate enough to get an actual officer on the line who helped me tremendously. Not only was he cordial and understanding of what I wanted to accomplish, but he also didn't belittle my interest in the paranormal. (Score one for that guy!) He gave me great directions and told me about the "hot spots" along the road so I could begin investigating right away and not have to hunt for a place to hunt. We discussed when the team and I would be arriving in town and he gave us all the "all clear" to investigate for as long as we desired. We were set to go! This was to be an official "Ghost Stalkers" investigation. For this particular investigation the team consisted of Emma, Megan, Kenzie, and myself.

The day of the hunt came. I couldn't wait to dive into this story and actually see where this bizarre tale unfolded. This was going to be good. I was going to be able to finally "break in" a new toy that I had recently purchased; the spirit box. The spirit box scans through radio frequencies at a very high rate of speed and uses the newly created white noise to act as a channel from which spirits can communicate. Think of it as doing an EVP session, only it's in real time. This makes it possible to hold actual conversations with the other side.

I arrived in Nebraska City and immediately contacted the police department to tell them I had arrived. I went ahead and went to the road to drive it in its entirety. This was an easy way for me to get the lay of the land and to identify the hotspots a little easier once the sun set. The team then arrived shortly after me. We met up in town and began to form a game plan. We gave the police the make and models of our vehicles in the event that they received any calls of "mischievous kids" or "suspicious behavior." That way the police could let the people know exactly who we were and what we were up to. All was covered. It was going to be a great night of investigating.

The sun was long gone. Night was in full force and had entirely enveloped the landscape. It was officially time start the investigation. I initially pulled out the spirit box, a K2 meter, and a digital voice recorder. I divided out the equipment accordingly and we all formed a circle near the right hand side of the gravel road. It was time to find out if the legend of the Seven Sisters was true or not.

Almost right away, we began to watch the all too familiar twinkle of lights bouncing from the K2 meter. This was an indication that a spirit was nearby. Almost immediately after that moment Emma, Kenzie, and Megan began firing off questions for the entity to answer. This is when I turned on the spirit box to have a little fun of my own.

After turning the spirit box on I began to receive responses to the questions the girls were asking. The responding voice was definitely a female and most certainly in distress. I found this to be interesting due to the fact that we were looking for one of the alleged sisters who met her untimely death along that same stretch of road. The only problem was that her voice wasn't clear enough to understand. We all strained a little closer to the device in my hand to try and make out what the spirit was saying, but we had no luck. Whatever it was that she was saying was that of urgency.

I wanted to help so badly, but we ended up losing contact with the female spirit.

"It's ok," Megan said, trying to calm us all down after losing contact with the entity.

"Yeah I guess so," Megan's sister, Kenzie was saying.

We all decided it best to travel down "Seven Sisters Road" a bit further to try another spot of interest. We piled into our cars and headed down the bumpy, gravel road for another mile or so. I was hoping that this would bring us better results than the last spot.

Again, we parked alongside the road, got out of the cars and gathered together along the right hand side of the road.

"Ready for round two?" I asked.

"I think so. I just hope we can actually make out a voice this time around," Emma was saying.

We all, again, brought out the "toys" and began another spirit box session. Almost as before, the K2 meter's lights began to dance around right away. This was a good sign. I turned on the spirit box and began to ask questions. This time, the predominate voice we were receiving belonged to a male. The voice was quite clear in its responses.

"Do you need help?" I asked into the night air.

"Not help," came the reply.

"What is it then?" I pried.

"None of your damn business."

That was enough for me. I thought that I may be able to offer some help to this spirit. Evidently, he didn't want my help at all.

It was at this moment that I was reacting to the last of the spirit's responses. All of a sudden a light shone from off in the distance. About a quarter of a mile away from where we were standing, sat a small farm house on the crest of a hill. This particular house had a deck attached to the back of it. On the deck stood a man. The man was holding a spotlight in his hand, and was shining the light in the general direction of the group.

"Just ignore it," I said, trying to be optimistic. Hoping to myself that the man on the deck would notice we weren't doing anything wrong and tire out.

The light disappeared. I had hoped that the man had had enough and went in to bed, or at least had called the police to report us only to realize that we had permission to be there. However, the man on the deck's plan was quite different.

We continued on with the investigation. Firing off questions left and right and doing sweeps with the EMF detector. Only a few minutes passed before the man on the deck returned with his handy-dandy spotlight that had to be a least a million candle power. Again, I told the team to ignore it. This was the time when the first gunshot was heard. The team and I jumped, obviously too startled to understand what had really just happened.

"Was that a gunshot?" Emma asked.

"Did he seriously just shoot a gun at us?" Megan was shouting.

"Get to the cars and head for town," I was yelling at the team. I had other plans in mind.

A second shot pierced the quiet night air as I was climbing into my car. I was so pissed that instead of following the rest of the team to town, I pulled into the crazed man's house. I was going to confront this guy face to face and explain to him who we were and what was going on. The only problem was when I pulled up to his house, all of the lights turned off. Apparently the man thought I was a moron or something.

As I sat in this man's driveway, headlights painting the whole darkened structure, I contemplated getting out of the car and knocking on the door.

If I get out of this car I'm technically trespassing. He could legally shoot me then. It could be worth it, just knowing that the world would be rid of one more slack-jawed yokel.

The only thought that kept me inside the car was that of my daughter. I couldn't do what I wanted to do, which was pound on his door and then pound on his face for a bit. He already fired two shots at us, what was to stop him from putting a slug into my chest? I was still sitting in the crazy guy's driveway with my headlights blazing against his house. I wanted to get out of that car so bad, but I just couldn't. Instead I did the only logical thing that I could do. I called the police; yeah that's right, the same police that gave me permission to be out on the road. They were all very apologetic towards me. They assured me that someone would be coming out to the house to talk to the guy. I explained to them that I wouldn't be around, and that I was heading back home.

I felt better that the cops were coming out to talk to the guy. But I really wanted to be the one to talk to him. I was still fuming. I did my best to calm myself down. I thought that I had let everyone down. After all, I was the one who organized the whole investigation. I was supposed to have all of this stupid stuff worked out. And this was definitely a first for me. I had never been shot at before. Never in my wildest dreams had I ever imagined that this would happen. All I could do was follow suit with the rest of the team and head for home.

A word to the wise: Just be careful. Good lord, I never thought that anything that extreme would happen to me. In hindsight, I'm sure the guy was thinking we were trespassers on his land. Regardless of the fact that we weren't on private property, we were on the damn road. I could easily see how we looked suspicious out there in the middle of nowhere. I should have knocked on every door of every person who lives on that road simply to make sure they knew who we were. I know better now. But don't get me wrong, he was also at fault. If he felt we were causing trouble he should have called the police and made a complaint. At least then the police would have been able to tell him who we were.

Bottom line is to use caution. We all got very lucky that night. The situation could have become disastrous in a hurry. It would have been a case when the *ghost hunters* became the *ghosts*. I almost shudder at the thought.

Chapter Nine

Nowadays it seems that there is a huge push for results within this field. Granted, we can't turn on our television sets without seeing something that would be considered "paranormal." It really has made a big impact on pop culture. But where does this put the paranormal field? Does it push us forwards or backwards? On one hand, there are now countless people who have found an interest in paranormal happenings and occurrences. Maybe they themselves have had an experience and want to get to the bottom of it. On the other hand, there are now a ton of "ghost hunting" groups that have seemed to have sprung up overnight. This isn't necessarily a bad thing. But what do they have to go on? They have watched countless hours of one of a thousand ghost hunting shows and think that is the proper way to investigate. Want to know a little secret?

There is no PROPER way to investigate. Not a single one of these shows has it completely right. If it were the correct way to investigate then they would get irrefutable evidence every single time. And, despite what the networks show you, this isn't the case at all.

Get out there and begin asking your own questions. Ask the questions how you would ask them. Investigate how you want to investigate and learn as you go. The biggest problem is people believe that there is a certain "ghost hunting template" that we all need to follow. But what makes them or their ideas any different than yours or mine? Nothing at all. Develop your own personal style of investigation. Take good notes and dive into the evidence that you collect with a fine tooth comb. But remember this; there will always be someone who can disprove you and your evidence. It's a natural thing. No matter how compelling your evidence is, someone can tear it apart. Be bold and be daring. My first book, "When Ghost Hunting Goes Wrong:

A Brush with Evil" is centered on a specific location in which I believe there to be a demon present. How many people out there actually believe in demonic forces? Not too many, honestly. But I wrote the book for me. I had to get the story out in the open and off of my chest forever. And who's to stop me? But there are a ton of naysayers out there who say that it couldn't have happened. The story climaxes with my friend being thrown out of a window. Is that fairly extreme and hard to swallow? Hell yes it is, but it happened. They don't know because they weren't there. All I have as my backing is audio evidence and the testimonials of the people who were there and witnessed it happening.

The bottom line is to tell your stories and get your evidence seen by people. Yes, of course people are going to laugh and scoff and call you a liar, but keep doing what you're doing and never quit.

Chapter Ten

So where do we stand with all of this? Can locations talk to us? This has been a burning question for me for years now. Why is it that I can't even catch a glimpse of any one of these locations without something stirring inside of me? The answer is simple, my friends. These locations, for me, have been the places that I have come the closest to actually touching the other side. Interacting with the other side. And communicating with the other side. The stories are personal, interesting, and sometimes; just funny as Hell.

One of the biggest questions I am asked as an investigator is: "Do you think we will ever have concrete proof of an afterlife?" The answer is complicated. I do believe that we are making leaps and bounds in the field as far as technology goes. But it is hard to tell if the paranormal is something that we will ever be able to actually measure.

Is it possible that we aren't meant to ever truly know what is to happen to us when we die? It is absolutely possible. There are many of us who agree that "the other side" is something that we will never be able to touch or measure. Not in our lifetimes anyway. Maybe the paranormal is something that we aren't meant to understand. If that is the case, another question comes to mind. "Why investigate it if we aren't meant to ever understand it?" Again, the answer is simple. This is my passion. I understand and relate to this line of work. I have lost friends and family and can empathize with the clients that are in the same situation that we all experience at one time or another.

For some of us, myself included, speaking with the other side brings comfort. This is enough proof to some of us that there is more to this life than what we are dealt. I have always felt that there is something after "this." This, what we call life. Call it an afterlife or any other thing that you please. I have always felt a strange draw towards whatever lies just beyond the veil.

I want to personally thank everyone for all of their support. I couldn't have done any of this without my friends and family in my corner. This is a tricky business. It's not the easiest thing in the world to approach someone and ask them questions regarding paranormal happenings. I'm getting better at it though. Most people nowadays know that I am an investigator and can approach me about certain things. This helps out a lot. It is also, no easy task asking questions to entities regarding their own demise, or why it is that they are still around.

I hope that you have found this book interesting. I also hope, more than anything, that this book raises more questions within you. Questions are what drive us all and make us hungry for answers. Thank you all.

Inscription for a Gravestone

-Robinson Jeffers

I am not dead, I have only become inhuman:

That is to say,

Undressed myself of laughable prides and infirmities,

But not as a man

Undresses to creep into bed, but like an athlete

Stripping for the race.

The delicate ravel of nerves that made me a measurer

Of certain fictions

Called good and evil; that made me contract with pain

And expand with pleasure;

Fussily adjusted like a little electroscope:

That's gone, it is true;

(I never miss it; if the universe does,

How easily replaced!)

But all the rest is heightened, widened, set free.

I admired the beauty

While I was human, now I am part of the beauty.

I wander in the air,

Being mostly gas and water, and flow in the ocean;

Touch you and Asia

At the same moment; have a hand in the sunrises

And the glow of this grass.

I left the light precipitate of ashes to earth

For a love-token.

About the Author

Josh Heard still continues his search for all things that go bump in the night. Since the release of his last book, "When Ghost Hunting Goes Wrong: A Brush with Evil," Josh has been the guest on many radio broadcasts and podcasts discussing his passion for the paranormal. When not searching for ghosts he enjoys playing music in the band JB Acoustic. Josh can be reached at joshheardbooks@hotmail.com or @joshheard1981 on Twitter and Facebook.

More from this author:

"When Ghost Hunting Goes Wrong: A Brush with Evil"

Available on:

Amazon.com Barnes&Noble.com iBookstore lulu.com